The Dead Don't Speak

A NOVEL IN DRAMATIC FORM.

The Dead Don't Speak

A NOVEL IN DRAMATIC FORM.

AARON OLSON

Also by Aaron Olson

The Kids From Yesterday

I t was an early morning haze that crept in the open fields somewhere in South Carolina.

Dark gray clouds swallowed the sky as it opened up with light rain, that trickled down on a man who stood in the middle of seemingly nowhere in front of a bus stop, waiting for its arrival.

He wears a red burgundy jacket and brown pants.

Roars of thunder crackle in the background. Flashes of lightning sneak through the thick fog. The man turns around to look out into the field. As more lightning flashes the bus pulls up. The doors open and the man turns around and steps onto the bus.

As he sits down all the way in the back, the rain begins to downpour.

While the bus drives on, the man looks out the window trying to look beyond that morning murkiness. He sees a couple bunnies hopping around that disappear into the haze while listening to the rain clatter onto the windows.

Sooner than later he becomes noticeably distraught. He looks down at the dirty floor and sees a couple gum wrappers, squashed soda cans and empty chip bags.

He begins to shiver so slightly. But not from being cold.

The light bulbs on the bus begin to hiss loudly. They flash on and off a couple times till they stay on steady.

A voice pierces through his head that startles him. He looks up to see a man in a black and yellow spandex outfit holding a bicycle helmet.

Something troubling your mind?

Grady gasps as he clenches onto his heart with his right hand.

Jesus! You really made my heart stop for a moment.

Sorry about that. I didn't mean to frighten you.

I'm sure you didn't. But where the hell did you come from anyway?

Excuse me?

Where were you when I got on the bus? I didn't see anybody.

I was sitting right here.

Right there?

Yes.

Well that can't be right.

Why not?

Because when I got on I gazed my eyes at every seat as I walked by. And not a single soul was to be seen.

I was right here.

Are you sure during my daze the bus didn't stop and you got on?

I'm sure of it.

Yeah. How so?

I saw you waiting out there by the field.

Right. Well whatever then. It don't matter.

Grady turns his attention looking out the window to see endless fields barely visible from the haze.

You never said what was on your mind.

My mind? What's it to you?

You seem like you got something on your mind that's bothering you. Something you need to get off your chest. And I'm a guy who is willing to listen to your problems.

And what do you do, go around looking for the first guy that's got a droop on their face?

It's a long ride. Would be nice to have some friendly banter.

I prefer to listen to the rain.

That is a mighty storm out there.

Yeah.

The weather report said it was supposed to be hot with rays of sunshine out there today.

Today has yet to come.

Judging by those clouds I wouldn't bet any money on that.

But I've experienced stranger things in this world.

Well good for you. Now if you wouldn't mind.

You don't like the company of others do you?

I like the company of others. But for right now I'd just like to listen to the rain. If it's conversation you're looking for I'm sure the driver up there would be delighted to practice the lost art of conversational intellect with you.

I'm not looking to converse with him.

Well I'm not looking to converse with you. I've said already.

Grady stares at Ed with tense eyes letting him know he means what he says. A few silent moments go by as we listen to the rain clatter.

When he feels comfortable Grady turns his attention back to the window. Ed continues to stare at Grady almost hiding a smirk.

If you like the company of others and refuse mine then you must be going through something.

Jesus. You really want to play bus therapist this morning. Don't you?

Like I said, it's a long ride. I'd just like to pass the time.

Why do you say that...a long ride.

We are far from town.

Bus takes about 25 minutes to get there. I wouldn't exactly call that a long ride.

Take the weather into account.

Even considering that. 30 minutes. 35 max.

Mm. Even so, that's enough time to get into it.

Get into what?

Your troubles.

Troubles? We all got troubles.

Yes we do. But I've got a hunch yours draws deeper than most.

You want me to pour my heart out to a complete stranger?

What's waiting for you in town?

Students.

Oh. You're a teacher!

That excites you?

Just surprising. But I suppose you do give off that failed writer now I gotta teach look.

Failed writer?

I don't mean to offend.

What's there to be offended by?

You weren't a writer?

No. I read the damn things but I would never tackle one myself.

So you failed before you ever began.

If you say so.

And what do they call you?

Thomas Grady. And yourself?

What grades do you teach Mr. Grady?

I teach English to high schoolers.

What books do you make them read? Catcher In The Rye? How To Kill A Mockingbird?

I do something a little differently. I allow them to choose which books they would be interested in reading. Only rule is that it must be literature.

Do your students like you?

Do my students what?

Do they find you as the cool down to earth relatable teacher? Or are you known to be the tough disliked one?

I would say I am liked. Maybe not the favorite of the school. But I do okay.

You're not aware of your reputation outside of class?

Now why would I know that. I don't go around looking for gossip.

Sure.

You ask a lot of questions. You know that?

Sure I do.

Well what are you after here?

I'm not after anything. I would just like to learn what kind of man you are.

What kind of man I am?

Yes.

What for?

I just want to learn what kind of people that walk this earth are like.

What does that mean?

There are two kinds of people in this world. Those that help people and those that run away from people. And I'm curious to the kind of people that choose to run away from a tough situation. How they could go on their days. Doesn't that make you wonder who those people are Mr. Grady?

Grady takes out a handkerchief and taps his face with it. Trying to catch any sweat that may form and drip.

I never really gave that much of a thought.

Are you alright Mr. Grady? You're starting to look a little blue again.

I'm fine. It's just a little stuffy in here.

I would suggest cracking open one of those windows there. But on the account of that hard rain out there, I would advise not to.

Thunder roars while a strong wind blows, knocking a few branches into the bus's window.

Leaving Grady to jump out of his body.

You a bit spooked there Mr. Grady.

I'm not spooked. Just a little on the edge. I got a big day ahead of me.

That I believe.

What's that supposed to mean?

That I agree that you have a big day ahead of you.

Right. Well if you don't mind me. I'm gonna rest my eyes for the rest of the ride.

But our conversation hasn't even begun to get interesting yet.

Interesting? What do you mean by that?

Do you always take the bus into town?

No. I usually drive.

Where's your truck at?

It's in the shop.

When will it be fixed?

They said they'll have it done by this afternoon...did you say truck?

You own a truck, don't you?

How would you know that?

I got a glimpse of it.

A glimpse of it? When?

Just last week. Don't you remember?

No.

The fog beings to creep in through the cracks and slowly fills the bus. It lingers on for the duration of the ride.

Don't you remember making your way through Oakland Drive? Sometime around midnight?

What is this?

What is what?

Who are you?

What happened around midnight last week?

How do you know if I was on Oakland Drive?

You have the answer yourself.

Did you happen to see something that night?

Like what?

I don't know. What are you implying here?

I didn't imply anything.

Quit playing games with me.

I just want to know what happened around midnight a few nights ago. You can tell me that. Couldn't you?

You saw something from your window? Heard a loud noise?

No, I was outside.

There wasn't anyone outside.

Oh there was someone. You know that.

What did you see?

Who was outside? I know you can tell me.

You got me mixed up with someone else.

No no. I have the right guy. I know I do.

If it was dark out and it was late you could mix people up.

Im sure Mr. Grady.

So that's what this is. All a big misunderstanding.

I don't think so.

Enough with the games.

I don't think you can handle what the truth is. I'm not sure how to even tell you this.

Tell me what?

Does the name Edward Jones mean anything to you?

He a friend of yours?

What I'm about to tell you will sound impossible but I assure it that it is true...I'm Edward Jones.

What do you mean?

I was the man that was crossing that crosswalk that night.

That doesn't make any sense.

Why doesn't it make sense Mr. Grady?

The man died.

Oh I know it.

You expect me to believe this? You're a friend of his, right?

You don't have to believe it. But that is the truth.

What do you want from me?

I just want to know what kind of a man can run a person over with their vehicle then leaves them to die in the street. I'd just like to know what kind of person could do such a thing.

You saw from your window didn't you? Heard the crash and looked out.

You have to accept that I was the one you killed.

You understand how crazy that sounds?

I do. But I can't express enough how true it is.

There's just no possible way.

I can prove it. You were there at my funeral. You hid behind a tree in the far back. You left as soon as they lowered my casket in the ground.

Grady stares at him frozen in time. No words could come out. His eyes wider than they ever been in his whole life. None of this was believable to him till that moment. He was certain that not a single soul saw him at the funeral.

How do you know that?

I know. You took great caution to not be seen that day. And you weren't.

Grady begins hyperventilating.

Stop talking!

Breath. Take it easy!

Stop talking to me!

Grady continues to panic.

You need to relax yourself Mr. Grady!

I don't wanna hear this anymore!

You can't hide from the truth. Just breathe and relax.

Go! You gotta leave me alone!

You know I won't do that.

Why?

You've done a terrible thing.

But I've never seen you before!

I suppose you wouldn't recognize me. You were too busy looking down at your phone. Tell me...was the message you attempted to read worth another human's life?

Stop this!

My life. Was it worth taking it for the message you were reading?

Bus Driver! Pull over!

What did it say?

I don't know what you're talking about.

Come on. No one is around to hear you admit it. It's just the two of us and the bus driver. And he's all the way up there. He can't hear anything.

Pull over! Please! Pull this bus over!

He can't hear you, Mr. Grady.

Why? What did you do?

Nothing. This is between you and I.

If I apologize will you go away?

Eventually I'll have to.

Are you going to hurt me?

If I were, wouldn't I have done so by now?

Then what do you want from me? I didn't mean to hit you! You came out of nowhere!

I wasn't out of nowhere. I was a quarter way through a crosswalk.

It was dark out! I didn't see.

Cause your head was looking down at your phone. That little device right there cost me my life. How does that make you feel?

You know I would do anything to go back and make sure it never happened!

That may be so. But that can't happen. You have to live with this for the rest of your life. Can you handle that?

Stop this please. I beg you.

All you had to do was call 911 and an ambulance would have been on their way. Probably would have saved my life. But it was real easy for you to just drive off like that.

I panicked!

Of course. Who wouldn't in such a stressful situation. But to take off? Only the lowest of scum would do that. Now how does a nice English teacher end up being so cold?

I gotta get off. Stop the bus! Pull over!

Don't worry about that right now. Just focus on me.

I have to get off this bus.

Oh you will. Just give it time.

Please!

What kind of punishment do you think you deserve?

I don't know!

How much is my life worth to you?

I don't know! What do you want me to say?

The truth. What do you think my life is worth to you?

I don't know.

Do you think you deserve to walk this earth freely?

It was an accident!

One that took my life! And you get to just walk around freely!

What is this! This doesn't make any damn sense!

What doesn't make any sense?

The dead can't speak!

I can Mr. Grady.

What do you want from me!

I already told you. I just want to know how a normal person could be so cold. What if I was someone you knew that you hit? Someone you loved. A wife. A son. A daughter. Someone's child. Would you still have run off?

This has to be a dream. I need to wake up!

It's not Mr. Grady. This is the reality you chose to live in.

And in this moment of time you're speaking to a dead man.

But how! You're sitting right there. In the flesh and bones.

Call it: Mysteries of the universe.

I find this hard to believe. I must be losing it.

How do you think your students would feel about you if they knew you killed me and didn't have the courage to stick around to try and help me? How do you think they would react to that?

What do you want from me? You want me to turn myself in. Is that what this is all about? A confession?

I just want a conversation with the man that took my life. Simple as that.

A conversation?

What was the message that diverted your eyes away from the road?

Grady puts his head down in defeat and rubs the top of his head. After everything that was on the news don't you worry they'll see that and put two and two together?

I don't know.

How do you think your students would react to the news that you ran from the scene? Do they look up to you?

Look up to me?

You're their teacher. Are you not?

Yes.

Don't you think they look up to you? At least one student?

Perhaps. But I never thought of that.

That's not why you want to teach? To feel superior and be the smart one in the room?

No.

You can admit it. Being a cop was too tough for you. You dropped out but you still wanted that superiority feeling.

And you got all this from what?

How was your high school experience?

Normal.

Define normal.

Just normal. You know.

No, I don't know. My experience is surely different from yours and our normals would all be different.

I don't see how they could be a different normal.

You see, in my house we had a no shoes rule. I grew up with that. I thought it was normal until I got a little older and started going over other people's houses. I took off my shoes and my friend

looked at me like my head was unscrewed.

Okay I get your point.

Do you now?

Yes.

So what was high school like?

I did my work and bothered no-one.

That's it?

In a nutshell.

Let's crack open that shell.

Look, there was no traumatic experience. I don't have this superior beast inside me. I was the quiet shy kid who did his work and graduated.

There's more to you than that.

If there's something you know, go head and indulge me. What is it?

I cannot say for you. That is for you to say.

Not when I don't know what you're trying to get me to say to you. You want me to have some traumatic experience for the way I am? You think people become teachers to feel superior? We become teachers to help people. To prepare them for the world. The next generation.

Can't you admit it makes you feel powerful being the smart one in the room at all hours of the day?

There is nothing to admit. What does this got to do with anything?

I'm trying to figure you out.

Figure me out? For what?

How a high school teacher who claims he wants to help students. Who wants to prepare them for their lives that are ahead of them and how you end up murdering a human. Leaving one to die in the street like a stray dog. Is that how you treat people below you?

You think I intentionally ran you over?!

Oh I know you didn't Mr. Grady. But what kind of person doesn't stop and get out of the car to check and call them an ambulance. Hell I get that you don't want the hassle of court and being arrested. But to not have the courtesy to make an anonymous phone call to get the paramedics on the scene? How cold is your heart Mr. Grady. How cold is it?

You don't think it's eating at me everyday?

Is it now?

Yes!

Well you know what you have to do.

I know.

But you can't.

I know I should.

You want that extra push.

My mind is too clouded.

Oh I'm sure it is...could I ask...are your folks still alive?

If they weren't wouldn't you be able to answer that for me?

But I'm asking you.

They're not.

Is teaching the career that you always wanted?

Of course.

What did your folks do?

They were also teachers.

You sure it wasn't brainwashed into your system?

Excuse me?

How old are you?

I'll be 55 in a few months.

Well ain't that nice. You think you'll live to see those days?

I'm fairly healthy for my age. I think I would be able to see those days.

Must be nice. Mm.

How do I know this ain't all just some dream I'm having?

You think it's a dream? Open that window, jump out and wake yourself up.

Maybe it's a trick and that's just what you want me to do.

You think that's what I want from you?

Is it?

Ed laughs.

Pardon me for laughing Mr. Grady. That is far from what I want from you.

So go ahead and spit it out. Lay it all on the table.

Are you a married man?

What difference does that make?

I just want to learn about you. See what kind of man you are that would leave a man to die in the street.

Stop saying that.

Did you think you were a hot shot teacher saving lives before?

I'd like to think I'd made a little impact on someone's life.

How long have you been a teacher?

22 years.

And you enjoyed all those years?

Can't say I have.

I thought you were proud to take after your family?

I can be proud and still feel unaccomplished.

Where did things go wrong?

I guess you don't really know if you make an impact on someone. You don't always come out with it to their face. There's been lots of people that changed my life and I never said a word to them about it.

Why not?

I guess deep down I figured they would have known.

Are they still alive?

No.

If they were, would you tell them now?

Maybe I would. Maybe it would have never mattered. They would have forgotten it the moment I left.

Did you know I was dead when you fled the scene?

No. I didn't know anything.

What if I had lived?

Yeah?

Wouldn't you have been worried I would identify you?

What are you saying? I should have made sure you were gone?

You've got quite a dark mind Mr. Grady. I was thinking maybe you would have attempted to get on my better side. Let me ask you. Have you ever actually helped a person before?

Helped?

Yes. Helped. You know what help is don't you? You are a teacher.

Like who? Helped who?

Anyone. Anyone that ever looked as if they needed help. A stranger lost in the street needing directions. Did you ever have the courtesy to help them find their way?

Yes. Of course I have. What kind of question is that?

I'm just asking. Cause to me it doesn't seem very much like you are the helping kind.

How are you here? I don't understand this. You had a funeral. You were buried. But here you sit. In the flesh and bones.

The world is full of illusions. Perhaps everyday the average man looks at a person never knowing they weren't even flesh and bones.

You're just trying to spook me. Right. That's what this is all about? Pretending you're a goddamn ghost.

Now I never claimed to be a ghost. I'm just a person from the beyond.

Explain that to me then.

Explain what?

The beyond. If you're really from it then go on and explain it to me. I'd like to hear that.

It's out of your reach. Incomprehensible to the human brain.

Well try me then.

I can't do that.

Well why not?

I just told you. Your brain wouldn't be able to wrap itself around it.

So what harm would it cause to just try?

It's something you could only experience for yourself.

You can't give me one clue of evidence you are dead as you say you are?

Lightning strikes and blinds Grady. When his eyes adjust, Ed is no longer sitting in the seat.

Grady looks all over the bus to find him. He checks under the seats and calls out to him.

Alright enough games. Where did you go!

He looks out the window. The fog is still thick as before and the rain is still coming down steadily.

He stares out the window and suddenly he sees Ed standing in the field in the distance.

His voice comes back.

_____

Do you believe me now?

Grady turns around to find Ed back in his seat.

You said it yourself. Life is full of illusions. So how did you pull that off?

I didn't pull anything off. You're capable of extraordinary abilities in the beyond.

This has to be a dream.

Are you going to do the right thing Mr. Grady?

What's the right thing?

You really asking that?

I know what it is. But I don't know if I can.

You've got no heart then.

I got heart. Lots of heart! You can't judge me by this! You can't judge a man by one mistake!

One fatal mistake Mr. Grady. One very fatal mistake.

And I would do anything to change that! To go back in time!

That's not the reality.

No. No it isn't.

There are still ways to do right by this.

Sitting in a jail cell is really going to help you?

It's not about me anymore. This about you.

Of course it's about you.

I know you'll do the right thing.

What else do you want from me? You want me to suffer for an eternity?

Now that you mention it. That wouldn't be such a bad thing.

I'm as evil as it comes then?

I didn't say that.

You said I deserve an eternity of hell basically.

At least a couple thousand years to burn.

Does it really exist?

I couldn't tell you.

Why not? Shouldn't you have those answers?

I'm not there yet. I'm transitioning.

And how are you able to talk to me? How can I see and hear you?

I don't have those answers. As I said before. They're just more mysteries of the universe.

Can you see other dead people roaming around?

No one's wearing a sign on their shirt that says they're dead. That's not how

this works. I don't know how it works. But I do know how it don't work.

The bus comes to a stop and the doors open.

Am I allowed to get off?

Of course you are.

That's that then?

We should do this again if you don't want to make right by this.

I gotta go.

Sure you do. But let me remind you, Grady. You don't want to do the right thing...well that is fine. But remember this. I will always be here. I will always be in your corner cheering you on. Reminding you of your failures. I will stand by you 24/7 just to live out my days through you. And I will make sure you have the worst nightmares imaginable. I'll make sure you wake up everyday in a cold sweat. Keep you tossing and turning all night long. I will be your devil anchoring you down day after day. If you could live with that. Then sure. By all means don't turn yourself in. Don't give my family the closure they so desperately need. Leave them mourning. But Mr. Grady...even if...when you surrender... just know that I'll always be around the corner keeping my eyes on you.

Grady stares at Ed for a moment processing what he was told. Then he gets off the bus. He looks behind him wondering if Ed will follow him. He doesn't.

Grady sits in the teachers lounge holding a mug of coffee. There are two other teachers there talking to one another. No one takes notice of the slight shake in his body.

The morning bell rings. Everyone but Grady gets up as he stares blankly.

He enters his classroom ten minutes late. All the students quickly stopped talking as he put his bag down on the desk.

I know I know. I'm late.

Where were you Mr. Grady? One student asked.

I had to stop in the bathroom.

Are you alright?

Yes. I'm fine. If you are all ready I'd like to pass out your tests.

Grady takes out the sheets of paper from his bag and begins passing it around to each row of students.

You all know how this goes. There will be no talking. No food. No whispering. When you're done, you will quietly bring your papers up to my desk then sit back at yours while quietly reading a book. If there are no questions...The test begins now.

As he sat down he looked out the window. The rain had stopped but something was making its way through the fog.

His heart began to flutter. He knew who it would be. Hoping it would just be his imagination running wild.

Ed stood out there staring into the classroom.

Grady stared back waiting to see what he would do next. In the corner of his eye he saw a student walk up and place a piece of paper down on his desk.

Are you okay Mr. Grady?

Susie what are you doing? The test just began.

It's been twenty minutes. She said with a bit of worry in her voice.

Twenty minutes?

He looked up at the clock with confusion.

Are you okay? You look a little...sick.

I'm fine. I think the coffee this morning was a bit stale. But I'll be fine.

You should see the nurse.

I'll be okay Susie. Take your seat.

He looked back out the window to find no one there.

During lunch in the teachers lounge he sat there staring at the wall with his eyes wide. Till his attention was distracted as Mr. Philips, the shop teacher, sat down next to him and put a can of ginger ale down in front of him.

What's that?

That there is for you.

What's this for?

You look a little ill in the face there.

Oh I'm fine.

Are you? Cause you don't look it.

I think I drank some spoiled coffee this morning.

Well shit. If you had it from here it probably was.

Yeah.

That oughta fix your gut right up.

Thanks.

There's also some crackers in that cabinet over there. You want me to grab you some?

No. I'm fine. Thank you.

Anything else on your mind?

My mind?

Looks like you're thinking real hard about something.

Just my stomach I suppose.

Well drink that there and you'll feel better.

He takes a sip. It satisfies him for a moment.

Could I ask you something?

Ask me anything.

Do you believe in spirits?

Like ghosts?

Yeah I guess.

Nah. Not much. I have an ex wife who believes. She would go around the house and sage it to scare off any spirits. Shit all it ever did was run me off.

Maybe you were the spirit?

HA! Now that's pretty funny.

Or the spirit was inside you.

Oh you're serious about this stuff?

No. I don't know. Makes you think a little. Don't it?

Well I can't say I ever really had an experience before. Something happen with you?

Oh no. Uh. I watched a movie last night. I had some strange dreams afterwards.

Nightmares can feel pretty real. I think the older we get the more real they actually feel.

Yeah. It got me thinking that maybe the spirits can enter our dreams or something.

Enter our dreams eh. Maybe you should talk to my ex about this.

I should speak with her.

Well you could. She's the lunch lady. You could probably catch her in the back.

That's a good idea. Thanks.

As he left the teachers lounge the lights began to flicker and buzz till they blew out causing a loud pop to echo.

The red neon lights for the exit signs were barely visible through the thick haze that came in like a whisper. A slight whistle of wind then made its way through the halls. Along with the sounds came countless floating bodies.

All had their own unique disfigurement quality. Some had their heads beat in. Others had limbs cut off. Other bodies looked like they were beaten in like hamburger.

One was completely unrecognizable as a human body.

Grady stood there in shock as the bodies floated past him.

The lights clicked back on and everything was clear. A teacher walked by and Grady stopped him.

I have a terrible headache. Did the lights just go off?

Yes they did. Just for a few moments.

I thought they did.

You should go see the nurse. You don't look too well.

I'm fine. I'll be okay.

Grady found himself in the lunchroom. There wasn't a single soul that was staring at him yet he had the sensation that all eyes were on him.

He awkwardly moved his way to the back of the kitchen where he found the lunch lady cleaning all the dishes.

Miss Landry? You back there?

Yes?

I don't mean to bother you.

What is it?

I just spoke with your ex husband. We had some interesting conversations on the topic of spirits and he told me you knew a thing or two on the subject matter. And that I should come talk to you about it.

Yeah I got my experiences here and there. Sure. What's the problem?

I just wanted a word with you about it.

Go on.

I'm having some issues.

Like what exactly?

Sounds a bit silly saying it out loud. But do you think spirits could enter through our dreams?

Of course they can. They can enter anything they want.

Are they all evil?

Evil? No. Not all. Most are there to protect you.

Is there a way to make them go away?

I'll tell you what won't. Saying a prayer. Don't even bother. You need a clean, pure, healthy lifestyle.

And they'll go away?

Maybe for a little while. But they could always be there. Once one sticks to you they tend to stay with you forever.

———————

I don't like the sound of that.

Why, what's going on?

I have reasons to believe I got a spirit following me around.

Why do you think that?

Gut feeling.

Has it done anything?

No...So there's no real way to get rid of these attachments?

Best thing you can do is go on with your days. One day you'll wake up and remember you haven't thought about it in a long time.

Something tells me this is much different.

Different how?

They're not exactly dreams I've been having.

What are they then?

I can see this one. Like in the flesh.

Are you sure they're not waking dreams? Flashes of images in your head?

No, I'm sure of it. We've had long conversations. Face to face.

When was this?

This morning. On the bus. He appeared out of nowhere. Began talking to me like he was just a regular guy then he hit me with it. He kept questioning everything. Trying to learn everything there was to know about me.

Why did he want to know so much about you?

It doesn't matter. I just want him to never return.

Mm. This does seem like we're dealing with something much bigger than just a vision or a dream.

What if this is a dream? Like right now. This moment.

That can't be. I'm well aware that this is reality. We're both awake in the back of the cafeteria.

That's just it. How would anyone in my dream know they're not just made up fragments of my imagination?

I don't think we would be having this coherent of a conversation.

It hasn't been long enough to get weird.

<u>Write your n</u>ame down.

Excuse me?

Write your name down on a piece of paper.

Why would I do that?

You can't write properly in your dreams.

She takes out a piece of paper and pen from her pocket and puts it on the counter.

Here. Write your name.

He picks up the pen and stares at the piece of white paper. His heart pumps faster and faster.

Go on, write.

Thomas Grady he writes.

See. There you are. I can read that perfectly.

What if I had the ability to write in my dreams? It's been done before by people.

I think you're overthinking this.

Or not thinking hard enough. I gotta go.

He runs out of the cafeteria and heads back to the teachers lounge where Mr. Philips is still sitting, finishing his sandwich.

Hey. You speak with my ex?

Listen, I gotta ask for a favor. I have to pick my truck up at the Auto Shop. Would you mind dropping me off?

The Auto Shop by Douglas Ave? Yeah sure.

Once he's dropped off at the auto shop he immediately walks up to his truck which is unlocked and searches for his keys.

A mechanic emerges from the fog and approaches him.

Oh can I help you there?

I'm looking for the key that belongs to this truck.

Oh Mr. Grady. We got your key inside. Come on in...Some crazy fog we've been having huh? Can't see a lick of anything.

He follows him inside.

You can leave that door open.

Yeah.

I can't remember the last time we had fog this thick.

Mechanic grabs some papers on the table and sorts them out.

Listen, could you hand me the key. I gotta head out.

Okay. Okay. No need to rush.

I need it now. I gotta go.

Now just take it easy. The total comes out to 2284 dollars.

The mechanic places the key on the counter with the receipt.

Will that be cash or charge?

I don't have the cash on me at the moment. I'll come back with it later.

Alright she'll be here waiting for ya then.

You don't understand. I need the truck.

Come back with the cash and I'll give it to you. Until then there's nothing I can do.

Listen, I'll go get the cash now if you give me the keys.

I can't do that. Just go on and get your cash. Come back and off you'll be. Till then there's nothing I can do for ya.

Grady takes a deep breath in and slowly blows out.

Okay.

He turns around and heads out.

Across from the shop is a gas station with a seating area outside. He sits down and stares at the shop.

Waiting.

After twenty minutes the guy at the front does not move from his spot.

Grady gets up and walks around the gas station so he's out of view from the shop to make his way to the side of the building where a pile of tires sits.

He forces them to fall onto one another causing a domino effect.

After they start crashing he runs to the back of the building to make his way to the front.

Everyone from the shop is now on the side of the building.

What the hell is this!

Grady quietly opens the front door and searches the wall for his key. He can hear the mumble yells of the mechanic out there till he gets closer to the front and hears him clearly.

Get that shit cleared up before you touch a single car in this garage!

He finds the key and sneaks his way into the garage as the guy steps back in. Grady opens the back door and runs to his truck. Turns the ignition and guns it out of there.

The students sat in their classroom waiting for Mr. Grady. They all talked quietly among themselves. Two students in the back sit quietly till one begins speaking.

I heard something happened to Mr. Grady. Ryan said.

Yeah? Like what? Greg responded.

He saw something. Like he might be possessed.

Possessed? By what?

A demon. I heard he ran in the halls like a lunatic. Thinking something was chasing him.

I haven't heard anyone talk about this.

We're talking about it right now.

And who else?

The word will get around.

Did you see something yourself? Where are you hearing this from?

You don't believe me? I guarantee you Mr. Grady will not be returning to this classroom.

Where is he?

I can't say exactly.

Then how do you know he won't return?

He's done a bad thing.

Like what?

I can't say yet. It'll all come out eventually.

Why are you telling me this then?

I'm just warning you.

Shouldn't we let the others know?

They don't care.

———

Can I ask? Where are you from? I never saw you take the bus or seen you around any of the neighborhoods.

I'm around. Near the school.

Which house? I live pretty close to the school.

Just around.

A sheriff and his deputy sit down in the teachers lounge with Mr. Philips and Miss Landry. The deputy writes everything down as the conversation continues.

So what's happening here? The sheriff said.

I dropped Tom off at the auto shop during break so he could grab his truck. And he hasn't returned since.

He didn't mention running any errands before coming back?

No. Nothing.

Did anything seem off about him today?

Uh yes. He kept complaining about his stomach. He was shaking a little bit.

Shaking?

Like small spasms.

What else?

Well he was talking about the dead.

What do you mean the dead?

Like spirits. He was worried about them entering his dreams or something. So I told him to talk to my ex wife here who is a bit more knowledgeable in the matter.

What did he tell you, Miss Landry?

He said there was a spirit attached to him. That it kept following him. Bothering him.

A spirit huh.

Yes.

The sheriff glances over to the deputy.

Like this spirit was talking to him?

That's right.

Mr. Philips you said his truck was at the mechanics?

Yes.

What was wrong with it?

I don't know.

He didn't say anything about it? Why it needed fixin or what?

He didn't say.

What kind of truck is it?

A 94 Honda.

What color?

Greenish blue.

Alright. We'll head to the shop and see what they have to say.

The cruiser pulls into the mechanic's yard. They immediately notice half the workers are cleaning up the mess of tires.

They get out and head to the side of the building where all the commotion is.

Evening fellas. The sheriff called out.

Sheriff. What brings you here?

Got a call about a missing teacher. Thomas Grady.

His eyes turn wide. Then he points with his finger toward the front of the building.

Come. Let's talk in the back.

The sheriff sits while the deputy stands in the back. Before the mechanic sits he offers a drink.

We're all set.

Sure.

When Mr Grady was dropped off did he seem off to you in any way?

Oh absolutely. Sonabitch was acting aggressive. If I were to guess, he was on drugs. It also appeared like he hasn't slept in days.

Deputy begins writing this all down in his notepad.

After he paid did he say if he was heading back to the school or that he had something else to do?

Oh he was in a rush all right. But for what I don't know. In fact he didn't have the money on him and stole the truck. Knocked all those tires down out there to distract us.

Was this called in?

No, I haven't had time yet. I've been dealing with that mess he left.

When did he come in to have the truck looked at?

A couple mornings ago. Maybe a week.

What was wrong with it?

Front end was bent in. Uh...a broken headlight.

What did he hit?

He said he hit a deer.

And you believed that?

Sure. Why not? Lots of deer around these parts. Seemed plausible.

Did you see which way he went when he took off?

Even without all this fog we wouldn't have seen anything. Knocked all those tires down. Got us all distracted. Snuck around, grabbed the keys and took off.

All right. Thank you for your time.

Grady pulled into a gas station. He got out and went straight to the cashier who was sweeping the floor and not paying attention to Grady.

Hey I'm in a bit of a rush here. I need a pack of cigarettes. Hey!

The cashier acknowledges him and walks over.

That fog is killer out there. Ain't she?

Yeah.

You said you need smokes?

Newports.

As the cashier turns around Grady grabs a bic lighter from the counter and stores it in his pocket.

Will that be all?

Yeah.

3.20.

Here's a five. Keep the change.

Grady grabs the pack and runs out while unwrapping the cart. Then he smacks the end of it and takes one out and lights.

Were you ever a smoker?

Grady turns to his right and finds Ed standing at the front by a stack of waters.

I don't know what this is. But stay the fuck away from me. I'm warning you.

Or what. You'll call the cops? Go ahead. I'd love to watch that go down.

What do you want from me!

I told you I'll be by your side.

Grady jumps in his truck and speeds off. But it doesn't matter. Ed is now in the passenger seat laughing.

Did you forget the abilities I now hold?

Grady begins swerving the truck all over the road.

What's that going to do? You tryna kill me again?

I want you out of my truck!

You think you get to kill someone and live your days as calm as can be? I told you I will make it a living hell.

The sky opens up and hail the size of golf balls slam down cracking his windshield. He swerves around the road again. Cars from the other end begin flashing their headlights as he is now in the left lane. They're laying it on the horn.

I can't see shit!

He spins the wheel to the left, landing off the road and drives into an open field. He looks behind him and the road seems impossibly gone.

Ed is no longer in the truck. Grady sits there while the hail continues crashing down. The windows continue to crack more and more with each landing.

In a few minutes the hail goes away. He turns the truck back on and turns it around heading back to where he thinks the road is. Only it never appears. He drives all over for ten minutes searching.

He decides to drive out into the open field. Going over bump after bump. He lights another cigarette.

After driving for a bit he decided to park under a tree as his eyes became heavy and began to rest.

Vivid dreams came to him in rapid fire. Dream after dream like a speeding bus passing by him. All bleeding into one another. He could feel his brain throbbing and kept telling himself to wake up.

The last dream he remembered was him wandering in a large open field. Sounds of summer nights were heard in the background. With clouds of mist surrounding him.

While looking up, the sky was clear for a moment as the stars sparkled unnaturally bright.

Carnival music rang in the far distance as he made his way through tall grass walking towards the sounds.

Up ahead he would see lights blistering through the haze. The ferris wheel rotating at an unnatural speed. Appearing in slow motion then erupt in fast motions.

Decaying flesh dripped in a flesh colored goop. Dripping from the bodies that hung from the ferris wheel by their necks in nooses.

Clowns with thin green balloon heads appeared from the mist hunched over scattering all over the amusement park. Blood trickled down their heads till their outfits were drenched with blood.

Grady watched as the clowns circled him. He jumped and grabbed onto one of the hanging men.

Climbing onto the ferris wheel as it made it's way up he looked down at all the clowns standing and waiting for the wheel to come back down.

He saw the entrance to the carnival and it read CNZLA NQSWLSF but in his head he told himself it read as: Carnival Of Souls.

Inside a barn the stalls were boarded up with cheap wood that had red paint splattered all over it.

While making his way through this, loud knocks came from behind the wood. Each bang felt like they were closer to popping out.

When he made his way to the end, the door was wide open. As he stepped closer, the outside became an empty black void. There was an ominous presence coming from outside. His body was frozen stiff to make any movements.

Something lunged at him from the darkness. Grabbed him and he screamed in terror as he woke in his truck. Trying to remember what it was that lunged at him. But he couldn't.

He looked out the cracked window to see the road was about 200 feet from him.

The radio was on and carnival music was playing through a scratchy static tone. He quickly turned the radio off.

A sheriff and his deputy stand in front of a door to a small house in a neighborhood. They knocked a few times then rang the doorbell.

We bustin in?

The sheriff peers his eyes through the window. Inside was quiet and very still.

I don't think so. Doesn't look like he's here. If you notice his truck is gone and there's no garage attached to the house.

Where to next?

Let's just get in the car and drive around some.

They get in and drive for a couple miles.

You think he's a guilty man now don't you?

I don't know what I think. What I do know is that innocent men don't run and hide.

Maybe trouble came to him.

I never knew Thomas Grady to ever be a man in trouble.

There's a first for everything.

There is.

We all have our secrets.

Secrets. I suppose we do.

What do you think he is runnin from?

I couldn't make up a scenario if I wanted to.

You never had a case where a teacher left for lunch to never return?

Can't say I have.

Do you know much about this guy?

Just that he's a decent, well respected man.

The sheriff stops at a red light and ponders in deep thought. When it turns green he's still lost in thought.

It's green, sheriff.

He averts his eyes back to the road and drives.

What were you thinkin?

Something I hope ain't true.

That bad huh.

Yeah.

You going to tell me?

You know that fella that recently got hit and died?

You're talking about Eddie right? Worked at that bar.

He points to the back of the car out the back window. The sheriff is too distracted with his thoughts to take notice of this.

It was a hit and run and they never found the driver.

You don't think Grady had something to do with it?

There was greenish blue paint on his bike.

Oh geez sheriff.

I don't know why I just thought of that.

We just drove by Ralph's Bar.

Did we? I hadn't noticed.

Poor Ed. My brother went to school with him.

He never married, did he?

Ed or my brother?

Ed.

No. Spent his time at that bar. He used to bowl every Wednesday at the North Lane Gutter Ball.

I remember that place. Spent a good chunk of my childhood smoking cigarettes in the game room. One night we even scored some beer. Saw the bartender pour the drinks. When he turned around we grabbed em and ran to the games room. Back then it was so dark and smokey they never saw anythin.

Simpler times.

That Sunday night before the incident, Eddie was standing outside at the back of Ralph's Bar staring at a pack of Cigarettes.

He began smacking the back end of it then took one cig out. He held it between his fingers for a long moment then put it in his mouth. He grabbed a zippo from his pocket and lit the cigarette.

Two motorcycles roared in the distance till they pulled into the parking lot. An older man came out from the back door with a drink in his hand that was half empty.

Eddie! Hell you doin 'back here? I need about four more refills!

The man laughs and smacks the back of Eddie in a playful manner.

Laura should be there. She's not off till eight. _____

Why you got that bum look on your face?

My ma.

How she doin?

Been a bit overwhelmed. She's been telling me she wish she painted when she had the chance. Had her whole life to learn before the accident and now she regrets it. Among other things. So the other week I surprised her with some brushes, paints and those half size canvases. She's been breaking down crying a lot this week just wishing she could see what the hell she was painting. It breaks my heart to see my mother like that.

I feel you brother.

And what pains me more is there ain't a damn thing I can do to help.

Hey. You being there for her means more to her than you'll ever know. Don't ever forget that. Don't be too hard on yourself. She raised you right.

I just wish there was more I could do.

I know brother. You hang in there.

Alright let's get inside. You really need that refill? Next one is on the house.

They head inside.

After his shift he heads to his mothers.

She lays in bed as he reads Of Mice And Men by John Steinbeck. Which was one of her favorite authors.

He reads the last line and closes the book.

I'm heading out now.

Okay sweetie.

I'll call you in the morning.

He kisses her cheek and heads out the door.

Outside he grabs his bike and peddles off.

While out on the highway Grady saw a figure up ahead and slowed down. He took notice of a few figures walking from the side of the highway that were coming from the woods. He slows down more to inspect what it is only to realize that these are people with rotten flesh.

Some have their eye sockets full of maggots. Others have milky white eyes that drip mucus.

They stumble their way onto the highway. He swerves and avoids them.

About two miles later he turns into a parking lot. There's a big red neon sign that reads DINER.

Grady sits down. An older waiter comes over.

You drive alright in that fog there?

Huh? Yeah. It was fine.

All my years I've never seen it last this long.

Yeah I don't know.

Well anyway what could I get you?

Get me a tuna melt.

Any drinks with that?

Cold milk.

While the waiter is walking away Grady looks around the diner for Ed. Or anything unusual. So far he's in the place alone at a booth by the window while a trucker sits at the bar.

Grady peers his eyes through the window. The red neon sign that reads DINER is barely visible from all that haze that just won't disappear. He thinks Ed is going to walk right out of that.

The sound of the cup of milk landing on the table takes Grady by surprise.

I didn't mean to startle you.

I know you didn't.

He holds onto his heart without realizing it.

You alright there? I didn't mean to frighten you like that... Should I call you an ambulance?

An ambulance? Why would you do that?

You're clenching onto your heart there. You got me worrying for you.

I'm fine. I'm fine. I just had a long day. Let me drink my milk.

He drinks. The waiter stands by watching.

You don't have to stand there and watch. I know my body. If I'm having a heart attack I'll go and let you know.

The waiter steps back and walks behind the bar and talks to the trucker.

That fella look alright to you?

The trucker takes another glance at Grady. They notice his body shakes like a spasm.

He don't look right to me.

He don't look right to me either, Frank.

I think I should call him an ambulance.

Did he order anything to eat?

A tuna melt.

Well I suppose you better feed him then. Maybe he's just hungry.

Alright Frank I'll go make his food.

The waiter comes out with a hot plate.

Alright I got your tuna melt right here.

He makes sure Grady hears him coming this time. Then he puts the plate down in front of him.

Is there anything else I can grab you?

That'll be it.

Enjoy.

The waiter stands behind the counter watching Grady eat.

Why you got your eyes on him like that? He looks fine to me now.

You think so Frank?

Frank looks over his shoulder then back to the waiter.

Yeah. He seems okay to me now.

I'm not so sure about that.

No?

I don't know. Something just feels off about him.

Yeah well people bring in all kinds of weird vibes these days. He's probably all doped up on pills.

The sheriff pulls into a gas station and parks at pump ten.

Fill her up. I'm gonna grab some drinks. The sheriff said.

When he stepped in he looked around scoping the place out. All he found were two teenagers roaming around looking at energy drinks and chips.

He grabbed two bottles of coke and a few bags of chips then headed to the counter. A young college student stands behind it.

Will that be all?

You wouldn't happen to know Thomas Grady, would ya?

The English teacher?

Yeah that's the one.

Yeah, he taught me English a few years ago.

By any chance did he stop in today?

I'm sorry sir. I just clocked in just a few minutes ago. Is he okay?

You see him, be sure to call.

I'll be sure to do that.

All right.

The sheriff sat back in the car. He took a big sigh and drove off.

He wasn't seen by anyone in there was he?

No.

How does a man like him not have a wife? Maybe there is something a little screwy with him? What is he in his late fifties?

Somethin like that.

You don't suspect somethin might be off with that man?

There's plenty of men that don't marry. Women too.

I know. I'm just sayin. He seems like the type that would have a family.

Family isn't always the primary focus in one's life.

That is true.

Best we don't speculate on the man. He could have endured some brain trauma and he doesn't even know it and is wandering around somewhere confused.

You're right.

Let's just keep driving and keep our eyes open.

They drive on in silence through the foggy town till the deputy breaks it.

I can't help but feel there's a nastiness in the air, sheriff.

Nastiness?

Something about this fog and the disappearance of Thomas Grady. It don't sit right with me.

Go on.

It feels like we've stumbled upon something much darker hidden in all this fog.

You sayin there's an evil inside it?

No. I don't know. You don't feel the nastiness in the air?

I do.

It's almost like the fog is alive.

It may be.

What if we stumble upon something we ain't prepared for, Sheriff? What if the fog devours us too?

You're spookin yourself.

I am.

Night falls upon them. They turn their bright lights on and make their way through the hills.

This fog really is somethin else. Isn't it sheriff? It just won't go away.

It sure is.

You ever seen it like this before?

Can't say I have. No.

Actin like it don't ever wanna disappear.

It might never.

Could you imagine that?

Imagine what?

Living with all this fog day after day...

I'd like to not think about it.

I'm gettin kinda hungry. You fixin for some food?

Yeah I could go for a bite.

You in the mood for some burgers?

I could go for a burger. There's a diner a few miles up here.

While finishing his tuna melt Grady looked up to watch the fog slowly creep in from the cracks of the front doors.

You attempting to run out of state?

Ed sat across from Grady acting like he's been there the whole time watching.

Are you going to bother me every hour of the day?

Oh I'm sorry. Am I an inconvenience in your life?

I just want some peace!

And I just wanted to carry on my days. Do you know why I was riding my bike at such a late hour?

No?

After work I spend time with my mother, who lost her eyesight in a cooking accident. So every Sunday I like to sit down and read books to her all night. When I leave I enjoy a nice ride around town. It helps clear my head.

Look, I'm sorry! I didn't mean for this to happen! I've done a lot of good in my life!

A million good deeds don't make one evil act alright!

Evil?! It was an accident! I never had the intention of harming you!

You didn't stop to help! That's the principle. You didn't even stop to call an ambulance. You made no effort into trying to save me! In my eyes that is evil and no different from pointing an unknowingly loaded gun at me and pulling the trigger! You deserve all the hell that comes to you in life!

To suffer in jail! That's what you want from me!? Just say it!

You deserve worse.

You're not even supposed to be here. You're dead. There's nothing I can do for you!

Grady gets up and grabs a chair from the high table and tosses it across the room hitting the trucker in the neck. He falls to the ground and begins to shake uncontrollably.

Grady runs and stands over him.

The waiter comes out.

The fuck did you do to him?

I didn't do anything!

He's all fucked up!

The waiter walks over to the phone and picks it up.

What are you doing?

Calling the police. What do you think I'm doin?

Don't do that! Hang that phone up.

Grady walks over to him.

Stay over there buddy. Don't step any closer.

Hang that phone up.

Come on. Why are they not pickin up?

Grady leaps over the counter and begins choking the waiter with the cord from the phone. The waiter tries to fight him off. Grady clutches his hands around his neck tightly. The waiter slowly passes out and drops to the floor.

He stands there looking at the two bodies. Unsure if they're both dead or alive.

Without thinking straight he runs to the back in the kitchen. He turns on the burners. He looks around and finds a couple towels and tosses a few on top of the lit burners. He grabs bottles of canola oil and squeezes it all over the ground to the front of the building.

Grady runs out and jumps in his truck and hightails it out of there. Smoke slowly makes its way out of the diner.

Somewhere along the way the truck ran out of gas and he parked it where it could only be slightly hidden from the main road.

From jumping out the truck he made his way through the woods where he would eventually see light coming through the trees and haze.

There was a decent size cabin that sat alone in the woods. He stepped onto the small porch that had an oversized pile of wood to the left that sat up against the cabin. While trying to control his breath he knocked on the door.

An older man with a thick beard opened the door.

You lost? This is private property.

I wouldn't bother you if it wasn't important.

You hurt?

No. No, my truck ran out of gas.

Do I look like a filling station?

I'm not from around here. I didn't know how far it would be till I found one.

So you go lookin in the woods?

Can you help me?

The man gives a subtle sigh and closes the door behind him. Leading Grady to the shed in the back.

You smell like smoke.

The man opens the door and walks in and grabs a small gas container.

This is all I got. It should be enough to get you to the nearest filling station.

I appreciate this. I'm sorry to be a bother.

Next time don't go rummaging around these woods. People live out here for their privacy. You lucky you caught me in a good mood. Otherwise I would have pulled my shotgun out.

I meant no trouble. I appreciate your kindness.

What's the matter with you? You doped up on drugs? Shakin like a bastard.

I'm fine. Let me get out of your business.

The sheriff and his deputy continue heading towards the diner.

You smell smoke, sheriff?

I think it's coming from the diner.

What makes you think that?

There's nothing else around here but that diner.

As they drive past the long winding road they see flames through the haze. They can feel the heat as they get closer.

Oh Jesus! The deputy cried.

The sheriff calls in for a firetruck.

Two men are outside the burning building laying on the

ground both alive. The sheriff and the deputy run out and attend them.

You fellas alright?

God damn hell in there! The waiter cried.

What happened out here?

Man went crazy and attacked us.

What did he attack you for?

God damn hell do I know! The fucker went and lost his damn mind.

Do you know who it was?

Just a crazy guy!

All right. Well sit tight, an ambulance is on their way. They'll be here any moment. Do any of you have any burns?

My arms.

All right. Hang tight. They'll be here.

---

rady made his way out of the woods. Behind him he noticed headlights seeping through the fog. He thought about flagging them down then something in his gut told him not to and decided against it.

He hid behind a tree only to see red and blue lights making its way through the haze.

A cop cruiser drove past him. He began breathing heavy despite realizing they didn't notice him.

He waited a few moments till moving forward.

A half mile later he was nearing his truck. Only he couldn't get to it. Two police cruisers parked around it while two officers were looking through the truck.

Grady stood behind a tree and watched them rummage through his things. He turned around and headed back into the woods.

Then he heard a voice.

Abandoning your truck?

You expect me to go approach those cops?

You're an innocent man. Are you not?

This is from you. What did you do to me in that diner!?

I didn't do a thing. You went mad. You burned it down.

I didn't go mad. You caused all of this!

He picks up a good size stick and smashes it across a tree out of anger.

This is all from you!

You keep making noise, you'll attract those officers. They're in range.

Don't jerk me off anymore. I've had it with you.

I have done nothing. Don't you understand this?

You said you would make my life a living hell.

You have done that to yourself.

He picks up another stick and slams it across another tree.

This is from you!

Up ahead one of the cops jumps in his cruiser and heads his way.

Shit. Shit. Shit. Shit! Now you done it!

Grady begins sprinting through the woods. The officer turns on his searchlights and points it directly at Grady.

He hears noise from the loud speaker but can't figure out what they're yelling and continues running.

The cruiser then high tails it down a dirt road. It continues till he reaches that cabin.

The owner slams the door open.

Lights on the cruiser shut off and the officer comes out.

Now what the hell is this?

Sorry to bother you Roger. We got a fugitive on the run who just committed arson at the diner.

Arson? You're shittin me.

I'm as serious as I've ever been.

I just had a fella come knockin on my door not too long ago. He reeked of smoke.

Yeah? You spoke to him?

I did.

What did he want from you?

He said he needed some gas. His truck ran out down there somewhere.

That's our guy. We expect him to come through here again. I'm gonna stay on watch. You stay inside but keep your eyes peeled for me. You got that?

I knew there was something screwy with that guy.

Grady watches Roger head inside and the officer flashing his light all around the yard.

He sneaks around to the bottom of the hill to the dock of a lake.

He unties the rope that is attached to a row boat.

As thick as the haze is, the officer sees him and makes his way down pretending he doesn't notice him. Roger comes out and joins the officer holding his shot gun.

There's no need for that, Roger.

You'll be regretting it if I leave it behind.

Grady grabs the oars, jumps on the boat and pushes himself away from the dock with the oar.

Get off that boat! The officer cried.

Grady rows as hard as he can till he slowly disappears into the haze.

You got more lights around here!?

I don't.

How far does this lake go?

Not too far. On a nice summer day you could swim the whole lake back and forth.

You got any more boats?

Just that one.

God dammit! I gotta call this in and get a boat out here.

Grady kept paddling. He was in the middle of the lake by now. Surrounded only by darkness and haze. The lights from the cabin were barely visible. He could no longer hear any movement or vocals.

The only thing he heard was the water pushing up against the boat.

Then he started hearing his own heartbeat.

Come out now. I know you're there.

He waits for Ed to appear. A minute or two passes but nothing comes.

Just make this easier for the both of us!

Still nothing but the water pushing up against the boat. The quietness is unbearable to Grady. As it makes him feel uneasy.

At times he feels he sees something emerging from the haze then nothing ever appears.

He looks up to try and see the stars. Only to be hidden from the everlasting haze.

Two hours later the sheriff arrived with two other officers with a police boat. The search lights on top seeped through the mist as they ventured out.

I don't like the looks of this. The deputy said.

They continued slowly making their way through the lake.

Up ahead the lights shined on the row boat that sat quietly.

The sheriff took out his gun and pointed with his flashlight in hand.

Come on Mr. Grady. Rise and put your hands on your head.

As the boat got closer they realized he was no longer aboard.

The sheriff took to his radio.

We need a team of divers and men to secure the other side of the lake. We got a swimmer or a drowner.

They stared at the row boat as it swayed gently back and forth in the water. Wondering what had happened.

By morning the divers found Grady's body. When they pulled his body out of the water and onto the boat his eyes were wide like he may have saw something unimaginable.

The sheriff and the deputy took a moment to stare at the body.

The mist was slowly evaporating. The skies were still dark gray yet had the feeling of light would soon seep out.

What do you think it was, sheriff? You think it was suicide?

I don't know what it was. Whatever it was, before he went, he saw somethin. Somethin we may experience ourselves one day. The face of god or the devil himself. I don't know what.

Jesus sheriff. What do you suppose made him go and do what he did?

Up at the diner?

All of it.

Who knows why anyone does any of the things they do.

You think he intentionally drowned?

Suppose he did. Or the fog finally caught up to him and it was just a slip. Along with other mysteries in our universe, I guess this one will stay with him.

About The Author

Aaron Olson lives in Smithfield, Rhode Island. To find more more information and see what he is up to next, check his social media sites.

Instagram: avoart_life

Facebook: Aaron Olson

TikTok: aaronolson_writer

Made in the USA
Las Vegas, NV
23 October 2023

79425085R00073